PRAISE FOR M

(Miranda Chase is) one of the most compelling, addicting, fascinating characters in any genre since the Monk television series.

— DRONE, ERNEST DEMPSEY

The first...of (a) stellar, long-running (military) romantic suspense series.

— THE NIGHT IS MINE, BOOKLIST, THE 20 BEST ROMANTIC SUSPENSE NOVELS: MODERN MASTERPIECES

Buchman has catapulted his way to the top tier of my favorite authors.

— FRESH FICTION

M L. Buchman's ability to keep the reader right in the middle of the action is amazing.

— LONG AND SHORT REVIEWS

The only thing you'll ask yourself is, "When does the next one come out?"

— WAIT UNTIL MIDNIGHT, ROMANTIC TIMES BOOK REVIEWS, 4 STARS

I knew the books would be good, but I didn't realize how good.

— NIGHT STALKERS SERIES, KIRKUS REVIEWS

CHRISTMAS OVER THE BAR

A US COAST GUARD ROMANCE

M. L. BUCHMAN

Buchman Bookworks

Other works by M. L. Buchman: *(* - also in audio)*

Other works by M. L. Buchman:

Contemporary Romance (cont)

Where Dreams
Where Dreams are Born
Where Dreams Reside
Where Dreams Are of Christmas
Where Dreams Unfold
Where Dreams Are Written

Science Fiction / Fantasy

Deities Anonymous
Cookbook from Hell: Reheated
Saviors 101

Single Titles
The Nara Reaction
Monk's Maze
the Me and Elsie Chronicles

Non-Fiction

Strategies for Success
Managing Your Inner Artist/Writer
Estate Planning for Authors*
Character Voice
Narrate and Record Your Own
Audiobook*

Short Story Series by M. L. Buchman:

Romantic Suspense

Delta Force
Delta Force

Firehawks
The Firehawks Lookouts
The Firehawks Hotshots
The Firebirds

The Night Stalkers
The Night Stalkers
The Night Stalkers 5E
The Night Stalkers CSAR
The Night Stalkers Wedding Stories

US Coast Guard
US Coast Guard

White House Protection Force
White House Protection Force

Contemporary Romance

Eagle Cove
Eagle Cove

Henderson's Ranch
Henderson's Ranch*

Where Dreams
Where Dreams

Thrillers

Dead Chef
Dead Chef

Science Fiction / Fantasy

Deities Anonymous
Deities Anonymous

Other
The Future Night Stalkers
Single Titles

ABOUT THIS STORY

US Coast Guard Rescue Pilot Sly Beaumont lives to fly. Saving lives off the treacherous Columbia River Bar rates as a really cool bonus. As are the fine ladies who flock to the uniform.

Petty Officer Hailey Franklin may be new to the USCG cutter Steadfast, *but she's a second-generation Coastie and knows all the guy's lines.*

But when a storm-tossed Christmas rescue throws them together, neither one is ready for the lightning that strikes.

1

"THIS IS INSANE!" HAILEY FRANKLIN SHOUTED AT THE STORM.

"When you're right, you're right." Vera replied from the passenger seat.

Hailey had met Vera Chu at the Portland, Oregon airport car rental counter. They'd gotten to know each other driving through the torrential December rain as they forged west to meet their new billet. Spending two hours together, squinting ahead into the darkness through the thick rivers that the windshield wipers on high couldn't clear, created a special kind of bond.

Their US Coast Guard cutter was berthed in Astoria, Oregon at the mouth of the Columbia River, which divided Oregon and Washington. And apparently it was crewed by fish who could live underwater.

"Perhaps there's a reason there are no scheduled flights to Astoria. Only a crazy pilot would fly on a night like this."

"You aren't the one driving," Hailey protested, not that she'd given Vera the chance. When she was in any car, she drove. Ever since her brother had tried to drive under a tractor trailer full of lobster pots and sheared the top off the family car—with her in it—she'd insisted. She'd managed to pull him down in time, so it was just instant convertible rather than instant death...but still!

"I expect this is pretty in daylight." Vera had spent the drive announcing views that her phone map revealed but the pitch black storm hid.

All Hailey had seen for the last two hours was slashing rain on the twisty two-lane Highway 30. Half the time blinded by oncoming headlights and half with her own headlights reflecting off the walls of water that the Pacific storm was throwing at them.

By the time they reached town, her arms were sore from fighting the wind as it slapped their tiny Mitsubishi Mirage about like a hockey puck.

They'd determined three things during the drive.

Vera, the tall Chinese girl from Detroit, was the classy one. Not that Hailey cared. She was fine with being the short black chick from the farthest butthole of Maine. Why wouldn't she be?

They were both USCG born and bred, on both sides of the family, and were both carrying on the legacy by having just re-upped for their second five-year tour.

And third, the chances were good they'd be spending this next tour together. They'd both drawn slots on the USCG cutter *Steadfast*.

She figured that was good grounds for being best buds. Vera had reached the same conclusion even if she was, like, so slender and forever-tall. Though watching her fold into the Mirage economy rental had been pretty funny.

"You're aware that our ship is based from here," Vera asked as they arrived at the town limits sign.

"Shit! I thought we were just going for a scenic drive to a total nowhere town for the hell of it." Not even Astoria was

2

as remote as where she'd been born. There wasn't a whole lot of America that existed east of Jonesport, Maine—the five hundred residents of Cutler and the Quoddy Head Lighthouse were about it. Maw and Paw had spent twenty years riding the buoy tenders along the coast and into the North Atlantic out of the USCG Jonesport Station.

"I'm simply curious regarding this place where we'll be based for a while."

"Won't see much of it. We'll be out on a cutter."

"This isn't the Navy."

Vera had a point. The cutter would mainly work the Washington and Oregon coasts, voyaging farther to sea only for search and rescue.

"Okay, let's see what we've gotten ourselves into." Vera had been navigator, not that there'd been any real questions. Out of the airport they'd had to make a grand total of one turn to pick up Highway 30.

There was a long silence. Long enough that the town lights were coming up.

"Um... As far as I can tell, the town is essentially one street wide and mostly in a two-mile stretch."

"Party town, whoo-hoo!"

"It means that the men are going to be small-minded provincials. Slim opportunities."

"Urban snob," Hailey teased her for her Detroit upbringing.

"Small-minded provincial," Vera teased her right back.

"Hey, just because I know how to haul a lobster pot and you don't, doesn't mean—"

"That's a pretty building."

"Columbia River Maritime Museum," Hailey read as they rolled by. "Could be fun."

"Oh!" they gasped in unison and Hailey immediately

eased over to the shoulder of the road, stopping in a deep puddle.

Just past the museum was the dock...*their* dock. A pair of two hundred-and-ten-foot, Reliance-class Coast Guard cutters bobbed there. Also, an old-style emergency lightship —the kind with a major masthead light that could be driven out to sea in case a lighthouse broke and couldn't be serviced immediately. This one was a museum piece.

"At least we know we're in the right place," Hailey had always liked the Reliance boats. They were the first of the post-WWII cutters. Built in the 1960s, they had a sleek, determined look that said they'd been the workhorse of the Coast Guard for half a century and were still up to the task.

"We're not due for a couple hours."

"Food!" They declared in unison.

Yeah, spending the next five years hanging with Vera Chu could be a good thing.

2

"You lost, Sly."

"Suck on it, Ham."

That was four times in a row that Lieutenant Sylvester Beaumont had lost the draw. He knew that his copilot Hammond Marcus was somehow rigging the game, but he couldn't tell how. This time it was their crew chief, Vivian who'd been holding up the chem lights, and still he'd drawn the red one.

Maybe...

He couldn't quite tell whether or not to trust her smile as she restowed the chem lights in their helicopter's emergency gear.

"Don't forget my horseradish this time, Lieutenant Beaumont," Harvey, their rescue swimmer called out.

"Blah. Blah. Blah." Sly had forgotten it once, like three months ago. Maybe it was Harvey's doing that he'd landed dinner-run duty four times running. The guy was quiet, but real sneaky. Yeah, perhaps it was *him* behind Sly's losing streak.

Harvey was sneaky in more than one way.

"Wedding just two weeks away. Got any nerves, Harv?"

"Not a one."

"Damn straight that better be your answer," Vivian paused in the middle of checking over her gear, long enough to pull Harvey down into a kiss. It quickly became clear that she was making it extra steamy just to mess with him.

"I'm outta here."

"About time," Ham grumbled.

Vivian's and Harvey's kiss broke up in laughter.

Totally messing with him.

He climbed into his pickup and headed into Astoria to get their dinner.

He didn't have a clue how Harvey had done it—and so damn fast. A total babe, Vivian had arrived on base last December 23rd. They'd been dating by New Year's Eve and engaged on Valentine's Day. Getting married on Christmas Day.

For himself, he had no real interest in slowing down yet, but he wouldn't mind that kind of lightning bolt striking him either.

And even though the Pacific Northwest wasn't much given to lightning, this Christmas Eve storm looked all set to deliver.

Wrong kind of lightning though.

There had been a pair of locals that he and Ham had been making good progress with—on that long-ago Valentine's Day. What with Harvey and Vivian getting engaged in their standard dive-bar hangout, it had set a definite romantic atmosphere for the evening—at least until Vivian had busted it up.

She'd sat down with the two hot townies and done the worst thing imaginable, told them the truth.

You girls want a good time, go for it. You want the long dream of escape from this town—because Astoria was the epitome of small town that most wanted to escape from—*Sly and Ham aren't your guys. The trick is, you've got to leave town yourself and go find what you're looking for. Take it from a woman who figured that out the hard way.*

And the two girls had. By the end of the month they'd both moved to Portland.

Vivian was a bad influence.

Vivian had made him think, though Sly hadn't mentioned a thing about it to Ham. Think a lot. (A *really* bad influence as that wasn't his normal mode.) And not exactly comfortable thoughts. What did he want long-term? Other than flying his USCG helo. What kind of woman was he actually looking for?

Damned if he knew.

3

"THAT'S A BRIGHT CHRISTMAS TREE," HAILEY BLINKED. THE thing was oncoming like major high beams.

Vera was doing one of her phone things. "Twenty-eight-foot artificial tree with four thousand LEDs in seven colors."

"Could use the thing as a lighthouse—for passing spaceships." Brake lights blanketed the road ahead of her. "What the hell? Who would traffic jam a one-road town on a stormy Saturday night?"

"That would be the Santa Swim."

"Santa Swim?"

"*Bring your Santa hat and float in our Aquatic Center pool for our annual screening of* Home Alone."

"You're kidding, right?" Then she thought about the blueberry costume parade for the Machias, Maine Wild Blueberry Festival. Maybe it wasn't so odd. Small towns did have their own quirks.

"There's also a Tuba Christmas concert tonight."

Hailey weaved her way through the traffic snarl and made it out the other side. "If we didn't have to report aboard, that would almost be worth it."

"There!"

The car rental was on the main drag. And closed.

They hoisted their sea bags (that they should have dropped off at the ship) and dumped the key through the slot.

Just up the street, there were a number of cars parked close together, lit clearly by red and blue neon lights.

They shared a shrug and trotted that way through the downpour.

"Workers Tavern. Known for burgers and prime rib," Vera somehow ran, avoided puddles, and read her phone.

"Sounds spendy."

"It…" *more* phone thing even though the door was like twenty feet away "…isn't."

As soon as they were through the door, Hailey saw why. The bar looked as if it had needed a major renovation—for at least the last fifty years. Someone had done some recent work on it, but not enough to make it look any better than a total dive.

Perfect.

"They appear to all be different currencies," Vera was inspecting an entire wall covered in hundreds of low currency bills that had been stapled there. Hailey could hear her dripping onto the old wood floor.

Hailey was too busy taking in the marine ambience to check out the wall.

Buoy Beer signs—must be a local brew she'd have to try when she wasn't about to be on duty. Oars, ship's wheels, giant stuffed fish, a couple bowling trophies, so many signs it was impossible to make sense of them—though "Play Meat Bingo Every Sunday" definitely stood out. Only one television, and it was off. Definitely her kind of place.

Battered tables to the front and a big U-shaped bar to

the back. Good crowd. Not packed, just cozy and friendly. Group of old graybeards at the far end of the bar harmonizing Christmas carols with no apparent melody and few discernable words.

By the amazing grilled-meat smell coming from the corner kitchen, they'd definitely hit pay dirt.

They dumped their gear and slicks in a corner that didn't look too grotty, then took a pair of stools at the bar.

"Beer?" The barman had a generous beard, shaved head, heavy earrings, and an impressive set of arm tattoos. He also stood about six-five and had a good smile.

"I wish. A Coke and a steak. Still mooing."

"Coastie?"

"Why do you ask?"

"No one except a Coastie comes in here asking for a Coke with their steak."

"Two of us." She nodded to Vera who ordered a burger and a pot of tea.

The barman just laughed and headed to the kitchen at the back of the bar.

"Tea, really?"

Vera just shrugged pleasantly.

4

Sly was so psyched.

Ham was totally missing out and he'd get to rub it in for the whole upcoming flight.

In a town not known for having a lot of variety—especially because their crew kept coming to this same place to eat and drink—there were two new women at the bar. With their backs to him, he took his time moseying up to the bar.

He spotted the luggage covered in slicks. Mega-bonus: they'd just hit town. Too bad he was flying tonight. Maybe they'd be around for a while.

One was tall and had straight, jet-black hair down to her shoulders.

The other, much shorter, clearly had curves, and super-curly hair cut short.

"Hey, Teddy," he sidled up to the bar. He handed over the order because he forgot to call it in. "And Harvey is whining about the horseradish again. Could you give me a container of mayonnaise instead or something."

"And mess with my man, Harvey? Dream on," Teddy grinned and headed back to the cook.

Then Sly turned. From the front neither bar babe disappointed.

As advertised from behind, the tall one was sleek. One of those Asian types—Chinese, Japanese, whatever. He could never tell.

The short one did indeed have curves, great ones. Lushly dark skin, and a sideways grin that said she totally knew that he was checking them out.

"His name's Teddy?"

"No, but he's built like a giant Teddy bear, so it works on him."

"Less than you'd think." The bartender planted a glass of water on the bar, hard enough to slop some onto Sly's arm—not that it really mattered with how wet it was out there.

Teddy's wink at the women proved he'd done it on purpose. Sly really didn't need the trouble and waited until he'd moved off to pull some pints at the other side of the bar.

"So, you here for the surfing?"

The Asian chick looked at him in wide-eyed mystification.

The curvy black chick almost snorted her Coke with a bright laugh, so he riffed on it.

"It's big here on the Coast. They even have an app that announces when and where the surf's up."

"It's December, dude." Her voice was low and throaty. Nice.

"Wetsuits. Year round. Honest," he raised a three-fingered Boy Scout salute.

"What? You made Tenderfoot? Can't believe they let you in at all."

"I got to Star."

"Oooo, Vera, we're in the presence of greatness. Too bad he flunked out before he made Eagle Scout."

Well, that gave him one of their names, but the wrong one.

"Actually, I had to choose whether I went Eagle or started lessons in—"

"Remedial 'Being a Human Being'?" She was quick.

"Yeah, that." He gave her a nod, conceding the round. — *flying lessons.* At least that's where he would normally work being a USCG helo pilot into the conversation. But he liked her quick response too much to ruin it.

It lit up that killer smile again. "So, you're, like, Mr. Surfing Man?" She held out her arms as if she was balancing and riding the waves.

"In this weather? Shit no. I'm not that crazy."

And her laugh gave him that round.

Teddy delivered the babes' dinners, so closely followed by a bag of his four orders that it was clear Vivian had called it in. Damn, just when he wasn't in a hurry.

Teddy tossed Sly one of those small plastic containers. "Don't be losing that, or you really *will* piss off Harvey and I wash my hands of whatever he does to your sorry ass. Mayo's in the order, that's his horseradish."

"Dude!" He held up a hand for a high-five, which Teddy ignored just long enough to make the bar chick laugh again, before delivering. Damn but she had a great laugh. Sly then tucked the horseradish container in his slicker's pocket.

"You going to be in town a while?"

"Yes, we are," Vera replied calmly before cutting off a bite of her hamburger—with a knife and fork.

"A fair bit," the other one mumbled around a mouthful of prime rib.

And for some reason he didn't understand, he decided to just play it cool. As if Vivian was watching over his shoulder and telling him not to mess this one up.

"Well, gotta go feed the wolf pack before they get too ravenous," he hefted the bag to make his point.

She waved a knife at him in goodbye as if he was totally unimportant.

"You got a name?" Sometimes you just had to ask.

"Yep. You?"

"Uh-huh."

"Good thing to have," then she made a show of sticking another bite of prime rib in her mouth before turning to her friend.

Only after he was out the door did Sly realize that he hadn't played his best card. "Coast Guard helicopter pilot" never failed to wow the ladies. Though maybe *not* with this one. She had a whole lot of different going on.

5

"WELCOME TO THE AVIATION DETACHMENT ABOARD THE Cutter *Steadfast,*" the captain had greeted them.

Then he scowled down at them dripping on his pristine bridge deck. The storm had abated enough that they were merely drenched rather than needing gills after the hundred yard crossing from taxi to ship. *Drowned rats asking permission to come aboard, sir.*

"I assume you know your duties when a helo is aboard. Chief Mackey will make sure you know what to do, otherwise."

That and a salute was the entire scope of their welcoming ceremony. The captain was definitely old school. *Yeah, just two new overeager petty officers to worry about.* With a total crew of only seventy-seven Hailey thought he would have at least asked their names.

The captain probably appreciated them arriving together as it saved him repeating his lengthy greeting.

After him, Chief Petty Officer Mackey, a taciturn San Diegan probably built rather than born on the Navy base there, had showed them where they'd be bunked together. As they dumped their bags, the chief had given the entire ship's tour—which had consisted of him asking one question, "Been aboard a Reliance-class boat before?"

When they'd both nodded, the Chief was nearly as brief as the Captain. "Good. You're the new AVDET team. Prior team rotated out this morning, so no handoff, but you know your duties. Stow your gear, get flight squared away, and then get some sleep." He'd know they'd both just crossed the country from Little Creek, Virginia, and Pascagoula, Mississippi. Which meant, on military transports that never connected the way passenger flights did, neither had slept in two days. Still, first priority was readiness. Sleep was a distant twenty-fifth on any action list.

Coast Guard cutters weren't big on sitting still and the two-hundred-and-ten-foot *Steadfast* was no exception. It had started moving out of port an hour after they'd boarded. Command must have said to start the patrol on today's date and the captain had interpreted that as straight-up midnight rather than daybreak. Hard-charger or total jerkwad had yet to be seen.

By the time they hit the flight deck, *Steadfast* wasn't so steady. She was nosing out of the Columbia River and into the Pacific. The last lights of the North and South Jetty were blinking away dead to starboard and port. Mid-channel markers slipped by in red and green. A peek over the side rail revealed nothing but churning waves.

The seas, which had been slapping the cutter side-to-side was now intent on porpoising her up-and-down as well. It took major waves to do that to a Reliance-class ship.

Full slicks, life jacket, and double safety harness, they'd split up at the rear hatch to survey the status of the flight deck.

Hailey uncoiled and recoiled a couple of tie-down lines just to make sure that the lay of the line was clean and wouldn't snarl if she needed them fast. She liked when she spotted Vera doing the same on the other side of the deck.

Together, they inspected the refueling and rearming status—everything at full inventory. Toolkit was good and spare parts were few. Made sense because a boat like the Reliance rarely carried a helo full time. She could cruise for eight thousand miles between resupplies, but probably rarely ran more than a hundred miles off the coast.

In silence, they did an FOD walk—more an FOD stagger, weaving like drunks back and forth across the pitching deck. No foreign object debris.

Because the HH-65 Dolphin's engines sat high atop the fuselage, it was unlikely that they would suck up any damaging debris. But the heavy blast of a helo's rotors could turn the smallest bit of junk, such as a dropped bolt, into a painful missile for the deck crew. Or even worse, roll underfoot at the wrong moment.

But the deck was clean, and they finally met at the stern rail. The thirty-by-sixty-foot deck was their main domain.

They gripped the stern rail as the bow nosed down into yet another deep trough lifting them several stories into the air. The lights of the four-mile-long Astoria-Megler Bridge, arcing high out of Astoria before touching down in mid-river to continue to Washington, was just visible through the storm.

"This is insane!" Vera repeated her call from the drive out. Now it was almost inaudible over the hard pounding of the rain, driven bullet-loud against the back of their slicks.

"When you're right, you're right," Hailey gave the same reply and they both laughed.

But neither of them moved.

For Hailey it was a blend of exhaustion and exhilaration. Maw and Paw had done their twenty years for the Coast Guard, retiring when she left grade school. They'd moved eighty miles south to teach at the prestigious Maine Maritime Academy in the relative metropolis of Castine— population of thirteen hundred plus a thousand students.

And here she was doing *her* dance.

As she watched the lights of their new homeport fading astern, she couldn't help grinning. Cute guy within an hour of arrival. Not too shabby. Funny too. Major, *major* points for not going for her phone number, or push for her name.

Like he thought they were fated to run into each other again.

The fates of her past had proved pretty damn fickle. The only thing that had held true was the Coast Guard. The men sure hadn't. She'd been hit on by married officers, too crass to even pull off their ring first. At least their new captain hadn't done that.

"Why do so many men assume I'm easy?"

"Looking the way you do, you're surprised?" Vera answered even though Hailey hadn't meant to speak her question aloud.

"What? Why?"

"Hailey. You're beautiful. I'm like this total stick figure of a woman."

"A totally elegant one."

Vera shrugged uncertainly enough for it to show through her gear. "I'm not the one he hit on."

"Mr. Surfing-dude Boy Scout? He's a total hound dog, couldn't you tell? That's what I always draw. Guy who falls for *you* will have a weak spot for pure class. I couldn't wear class even if it came in a dress my size. And trust me, it doesn't."

"So, what happens if you run into him again?"

"Not gonna happen. We're headed out on patrol."

Vera's shrug this time indicated something else, but Hailey wasn't sure what.

6

"Thursday. This has gotta be a Thursday."

"It's Tuesday. You and I go off rotation on Thursday."

"Oh, that's why I always thought Thursdays sucked. You sure this isn't a Thursday?" Sly would *always* rather be flying—except maybe tonight. The hangar's inside worklights barely made it out the door. Beyond the windshield of his US Coast Guard HH-65 Dolphin helicopter the sideways rain slashed even harder off the Pacific than when he'd done their dinner run. As the engines continued spinning up, he decided that the night looked very, very Thursdayish no matter what Ham said.

Air Station Astoria was defended from the direct onslaught of the Pacific storms which slammed the Oregon Coast by sitting three miles inland. The problem was that the high point in that three miles was all of eight feet above sea level. The airport lifted a full yard higher into the wind at eleven feet. The stunted coastal pines had been kept well back from the west side of the airport, so offered little defense.

"The storms know, they just know." He continued

checking the items on the pre-takeoff checklist as Ham called them out from the copilot's seat.

"Know what? N1 at release?"

"Starter released. They know just how to swing into the mouth of the Columbia River so they can hit us with a straight shot."

"You're now manifesting this poor, little, innocent storm with evil intelligence to make up for your weird Gloucester Nor'easter superstitions? You're a real sad dude, Sly. Engine and transmission oil?"

"Check and rising. Just like this damn storm's temper. Innocent, my butt. Why do people have to go out to sea and get in trouble on nights like this? Why can't they just all stay home?" Sly could hear his past sneaking into his own voice. He still remembered the nine days huddled with Mom until they'd found Dad's fishing boat—or what was left of it—washed up on the remote Sober Island along Nova Scotia. "Unlikely-sober" Island as Mom had called it ever since.

Tonight, the inevitable call came in: crab boat in the shit —and sinking.

"Because if they did, we'd be out of a job. Nav lights, caution breaker, fuel boost?"

"On, in, and in," Sly tapped each switch and circuit breaker to confirm it and kept his tone light. "You're right. That would be even worse. Then who would pay us to fly?"

"Well, no one would pay *you*. But I'm such a handsome and charming brother, they'd keep me on just to make the Coast Guard look good."

"The only way you'd ever look good, Ham, is if they slipped a different corpse in your casket after you died." There'd been a debate ever since they'd hit the same air station on the same day two years back: which of them drew in the women, and which repelled them. Their far superior success as a team made it difficult to keep any meaningful score—not that it stopped them from trying.

He'd long since learned that pointing out his last name, Beaumont, meant "pretty mountain" was a bad idea. *Talk about mountains out of molehills,* Ham had instantly replied. *You know, you do kinda look like a mole.* Yeah, so not worth the effort. And he couldn't do much with Ham's last name of Markson. And he was a damned handsome black dude. He'd have to make sure *not* to introduce him to the sassy girl in the bar if he did manage to run into her again.

They were all the way down to anti-ice system check, which they'd be bound to need in the December storm, before Ham tried again.

"ELT check? We gotta watch the bar."

Sly glanced over. How could Ham know about the total babe? He hadn't been there.

Oh, the Bar (Captial B). The Columbia River Bar.

"Check." As always, he sent up a brief prayer to Mama's God asking that they wouldn't need the Emergency Location Transmitter tonight. It would only be needed if they crashed.

The mouth of the Columbia River Bar was also known as the Graveyard of the Pacific. The worst and most dangerous stretch of shipping water anywhere in the world. Even the Straits of Magellan at the southern tip of Chile were more traversable. They also had a lot less traffic, instead of servicing three of the top fifteen US agricultural ports like the Columbia. Not to mention enough recreational boaters to make a man choke on his soda.

"Yeah, the Bar." On a night like this—with the Columbia dumping two million gallons of water per second into the ocean, and the storm surge, not to mention the high tide ignoring all that to try for Portland way upriver—there was bound to be some major ugliness. Except the call had come in from much farther out to sea.

"Instruments all normal?"

There was a long silence as they both double-checked for any bad instrument readings—from compass to engine temperature to altimeter (which revealed a depressingly low barometric reading for eleven feet above sea level). There weren't any problems because the Dolphin was an awesome search-and-rescue helo.

"All normal," Sly reported per the checklist then called back over the intercom. "You two still with us?"

Harvey the rescue swimmer grunted an affirmative. Guy hadn't even tasted the mayo. He'd taken one look at it, then held out his hand until Sly placed the horseradish container in his palm. He'd now be belted in at the very rear of the cargo cabin.

Vivian's seat placed her facing backward directly behind his own position. She reported by the numbers because she was that kind of squared-away gal.

"Wedding is Christmas Day. Can we trust the two of you to keep your hands off each other back there?"

"Can we trust you two to keep *your* hands off each other?" Vivian shot back.

"Only because it takes two hands to fly," Harvey offered one of his rare comments.

"It's Sly," Ham joined in. "He can't stand that I'm the pretty one."

"Just get us out there," Vivian gave a long-suffering sigh.

"Your wish is my command, oh Queen of the Skies."

He eased up on the collective, rocked the cyclic forward, and climbed up into the darkening sky.

7

"HOW LONG WERE WE ASLEEP?" VERA GROANED.

Hailey checked her watch and sighed, but put on her most cheerful tone. "Almost two hours. What's your problem, Vera?"

"I'm not some android like you is the problem. I need at least two-and-a-half hours to recharge my batteries."

They dressed fast and reported to the bridge as ordered.

Despite the late hour, the captain was on deck. As well as the XO, two helmsmen, a navigator, and a radio operator. Chief Mackey arrived moments later.

The captain waved them over to the chart table.

"Franklin. Chu. Glad to see you're not sickers."

So, the fact that they didn't puke in bad weather had earned them "named" status in the captain's book. Hailey was okay with that. Because if the Reliance had been lively before, now she was positively active. Quartering waves, with the engines now running at full turns based on the vibration through Hailey's boot soles, gave the *Steadfast* a funky, hip-hop beat motion—one that Hailey's Maine heritage had never been able to follow on the dance floor. However, on a boat? No prob.

"We're in pursuit of the *Savannah Jack*. Forty-six-foot aluminum crabbing boat that's lost its engines and is in imminent peril of sinking. Crew of five. She's over two hundred miles out."

Mackey cursed, "How the hell did they end up that far offshore?"

"Unclear. Drunk, asleep, driving for Alaska in too small a boat? Who knows. We will *not* arrive in time."

That earned him silence.

"There's an HH-65 Dolphin enroute. Our mandate is to get as close as we can to serve as a landing platform."

Hailey didn't have to do the math. Vera's look said she'd reached the same conclusion.

A four-hundred-mile round trip was close to the helicopter's total range. If they had to linger onsite for a rescue, they wouldn't get back to land. Every mile closer the cutter could get to the crabber was that much longer the helo could remain on-station at the sinking.

"We've checked over everything on the flight deck, sir. We're as ready as we can be for a landing in this kind of weather."

"You will not be losing me a helo on your first day. Are we clear on that?"

"Yes, sir," she and Vera snapped it out in unison.

"Then we understand each other. I let you sleep as long as I could. The helo is already at the *Savannah Jack*. They were able to locate her immediately thanks to the crabber having an ELT. We'll be out past fifty miles by the time the helo will be coming back. They're winching aboard the last crewman and the helo's swimmer right now."

"Must be hell out there," Mackey grumbled.

There was a brief silence as they all sent prayers or whatever was needed out to the rescue swimmer down in that turbulent mess.

"They'll be here in under an hour. Recruit whoever you need, get them safely onto my deck."

"Yes sir."

"I'll send you a pair of MEs," Mackey said before waving them aft. Maritime Law Enforcement Specialist meant a sailor who was good at thinking fast on their feet in chaotic environments.

Hailey could get to like Mackey.

8

"WELL, THAT WAS FUN," HAM ANNOUNCED.

Even with the two of them and the four-axis autopilot the rescue had been a major battle. Even clear of the land effects, the waves and wind had been in a contrary mood.

Harvey and Vivian had done their usual amazing task. Harvey had dived into the fray, eventually recovering two bodies and three survivors. While they worked frantically to save the latter from hypothermia, it was now up to Sly to get them to the cutter *Steadfast*. Quickly.

But getting there fast wasn't the problem. They had a ferocious tailwind, which was a good thing. If it had been a headwind, as it had on the way out, they would be in even worse trouble than they were. Having his only available refuge being a hard-pitching cutter just five times longer than his helo was not a comfortable thought tonight.

"Cutter *Steadfast*. This is Dolphin 58 inbound," Ham called ahead on the radio.

"Roger, 58. Winds forty, gusting sixty. Waves at thirty, chaotic." *That* was the problem. Landing on the pitching helo deck.

"Roger that. We'll need immediate medical for the three survivors. Crew plus five aboard." A nice way to say they had two in body bags.

"Sounds like this is going to be even *more* fun." Sly couldn't see a thing out in the utterly foul night and was completely dependent on instruments. Storm dark. Moonless storm dark. And they were still fifty miles to the ship.

"Sure thing. And I'm not looking for a swim, so try actually landing on the deck this time."

Back during training, Sly had misread the markers on the airport runway that were supposed to be the outline of a ship's deck. So, he'd landed *beside* the theoretical ship rather than *on* it. Five years, and Ham hadn't let him off the hook on that yet. "It was my first landing, for crying out loud."

"Whine. Whine. Whine," Ham teased as he entered *Steadfast's* latest GPS coordinates into the onboard systems. "Fifteen minutes," he called back to Vivian and Harvey.

"Okay," Vivian's calm response was a good sign for the three survivors. Not that she was ever *not* calm. But if things were still going badly, she'd be too focused to even hear them.

"Man, that's gotta be a rough ride. *Steadfast* is coming toward us at full steam."

Sly eyed the fuel gauges and hoped that she really was. He had reserve fuel, but he'd have to land dead clean if he didn't want to get caught depending on it.

He hoped he could make it back to shore tonight. Maybe swing by the Workers and see if the nameless woman was still there, crooked smile and all. Wicked hot, but...he hadn't really looked at her body once he'd heard her laugh. Weird thing to stick in his head. He hadn't even lorded their meeting over Ham, which was not like him at all.

Whoever she is someday, Sylvester, Mom was the only one to always use his full name, *make sure she's someone who does not go to sea.* She'd never really recovered from Dad going down. Of course, Sly couldn't imagine anyone being prouder or bragging more on her son, than when he'd qualified as a helo pilot for the Coast Guard.

Or more afraid.

9

WITH THE PERIMETER FENCE AROUND THE FLIGHT DECK folded down and Astoria nowhere in sight, Hailey felt a hundred times more exposed.

Her first tour had been out of Virginia Beach, Virginia. She'd ridden out some rough storms—tail ends of hurricanes and such. But Mackey had said that tonight was nothing out of the ordinary. *Just five thousand miles of open Pacific come to piss on us.*

Clearly, this posting was going to have a whole lot of new experiences for her.

Experiences like the guy in the bar?

Vera had only brought him up about six more times—in that quiet way of hers. As if Hailey wasn't thinking of him enough on her own.

She'd lived in enough small towns to see how completely he stood out in the crowd. Hell, he'd stand out in any crowd.

Hailey again checked the deck. Between them, she and Vera had decided to take turns as the lead Landing Director.

She'd immediately claimed first right by order of the alphabet.

"Hailey wins out over Vera."

"What about Chu over Franklin?"

"H plus F equals eighth plus sixth letter of the alphabet. V for Vera plus anything is like a kajillion. My win."

Now she stood at the forward end of the open flight deck and wished she'd gone second. Tonight's landing on the pitching deck was going to be a nightmare.

Vera stood off to the side with a pair of unlit batons just as backup. The two MEs were squatting off to either side. They knew the drill, but she and Vera had gone over it with them again anyway. They'd spent half an hour talking through escape routes if something went wrong, firefighting in case whatever it was went *badly* wrong, and every other scenario she could come up with. Besides, it beat the hell out of waiting and wishing she was still asleep.

"This is Dolphin 58. Have you in sight, *Steadfast,*" sounded over the radio headset built into her safety helmet.

"Say again," Hailey couldn't believe it. She knew that voice, but couldn't place from where. She hadn't heard of any of the guys from her last station at Virginia Beach transferring out West. No, it was more recent than that.

Swiveling around, she spotted the helo coming to hover off the port side.

"Belay that. Roger in sight."

Not quite hover, as the ship would be driving ahead at fifteen knots and the wind blowing the other way at forty-plus. He was actually flying at sixty knots and looked as if he'd been bolted into place against the vast blackness. The pilot was so steady that it was the first time she was really aware of how badly the deck was heaving about.

Her body knew what to do with the pitching deck, but her eyes tracking the helo back and forth were less sure.

"Captain, are we dead into the wind?"

For the moment, she was the master of the ship.

"If this wind *has* a dead into, we're there," he called back. She could feel him up on the bridge, maybe out on a wing in the storm, watching his newest crews' every move.

She glanced behind her to make sure that she was exactly in front of the foot-wide yellow stripe painted up the aftmost bulkhead. It marked the center of the ship and the center of the Flight Deck for the pilot.

A hard gust and her gut told her that the boat had just made a fierce twist from slamming a wave.

Just gotta surf it smooth.

And then she knew exactly where she'd heard the pilot's voice before.

10

THE LAUGH OVER SLY'S HEADSET WAS AS BRIEF AS IT WAS unique.

"You've got a sick idea of fun, Ham."

But it wasn't Ham's laugh.

Sly had never put down on a deck when a ship was as breezed up as the *Steadfast* was doing. This was gonna be savage.

He briefly wondered if the nameless woman in the bar danced. He sure hoped so. She'd be something to watch.

And she'd have a laugh like...

"Ha!"

"What?"

"Nothing, Ham. Tell you the joke later.

Green baton pointed to the left, the deck crewman—the nameless bar girl, new to town, USCG new to the *Steadfast* (damn but that *was* really funny)—began waving him inboard with the red.

He shuffled over until the yellow stripe was dead ahead. The problem—that the H at the center of the helipad was rockin' and rollin'—was the baton wielder's problem.

For now, he set aside everything except what she was signaling for him to do. It was one of the hardest things for any pilot. He could see the boat pitching, but he'd never be able to anticipate it well enough to land.

This required absolute trust in the person on deck guiding him in.

Sly shoved aside how much he didn't know about the woman, he locked his attention on staying centered on that yellow stripe of the ship's mid-line, and focused on her two batons.

Down...hold!

Hold.

Hold.

Down! Hold!

He found her rhythm easy to follow.

Batons out to her sides and then angled down when he could descend.

Swinging level to hold.

Only twice did she have to signal him to climb, with upraised batons.

"He's good," Ham mumbled somewhere in the background.

She, but Sly kept that to himself.

The trick was to descend until he was just above the highest point the deck ever swung. Then to be there—the exact moment it swung to its peak.

Down! Hold. Down! Hold.

He could feel the tension between them, the perfect synchronicity of their mutual dance the moment before she gave the final signal.

Two batons straight down.

Sly shoved the collective down. If the ship was in the

wrong place by so much as five feet he could pitch to the deck, shatter his rotors, maybe even be thrown overboard.

The wheels didn't even slam down onto the deck. She'd gotten him so perfectly positioned that he kissed down on it.

Following her direction, he pushed the rotor full down, creating negative lift, pinning the helo to the deck.

The disadvantage was that negative lift would drag the tips of the whirling main rotor blades dangerously low.

But he saw the deck crew scramble for the tie-downs practically on all fours. Well-rehearsed.

In less than thirty seconds, she crossed the batons in front of her chest, giving him the Cut Engines sign.

Just before she did, she held the batons out front and back, level for just an instant.

"What the hell is that sign?" Ham asked him.

"Surfin', dude. She's surfin'."

11

HAILEY TRIED TO FIGURE OUT JUST WHAT WAS HAPPENING, BUT couldn't seem to.

Workers Tavern was packed to the gills.

The Christmas Day wedding had been at the community pool. She supposed it made sense for the wedding of a rescue swimmer, but it was still weird to have the wedding party all in the pool and the bride and groom up on the diving board.

Weird in a gloriously small-town-funny way that she totally dug. The bride's high-brow mom hadn't looked terribly amused, but everyone else was having too much fun to care.

Hailey loved that her bikini had gobsmacked Sly Beaumont straight into stuttering silence.

Vera's shy streak wasn't doing much at fending off a whole lot of male attention. She had looked so perfect in her sleek one-piece that all the guys were hovering, including Sly's copilot.

Most of her crew had returned to the cutter. The captain had said that he wanted at least one of his AVDET people on the boat before midnight—which actually felt pretty damn good. He'd complimented them both on a difficult task well done and it felt as if they really were a part of the team already. It boded well for the five years to come.

"This is insane!" Vera had whispered as she begged off before the party shifted from the pool to the tavern.

"When you're right, you're right," Hailey had hugged her tightly g'night before following Sly to Workers for the wedding dinner and dancing. The latest deluge was so cold after the warm pool that laughter had been the only answer.

It *was* insane.

She'd known Vera and Sly for two whole weeks. And it felt as if she'd never had a closer friend or known any man better.

Now she and Sly were boogieing down to a small up-tempo band, with the four graybeards as backup vocals inventing any melodies they didn't already know—which was most of them.

The giant bartender, in an equally giant Santa suit, handed out eggnog and hearty calls of, "Ho! Ho! Ho!"

Hailey missed when she and Sly switched from dancing with the beat to... The transition from rocking out with Sylvester Beaumont to slow-dancing curled up against his chest had passed without notice. It was just so natural.

For a while, she just let herself soak in how good it felt. *He* felt. No man had ever felt this way.

And somehow it didn't surprise. Everything about Sylvester Beaumont felt easy and natural. The teasing in the bar. The perfect synchronicity during the helo's landing—he'd been masterful. Then they'd talked for hours and hours aboard the cutter despite her exhaustion, and more when they were both ashore, with flirtatious emails in between.

The twinkle lights strung from the ceiling fans... twinkled. The graybeard quartet actually found the harmony on *I Saw Mommy Kissing Santa Claus*. The laughter rippled around the bar in a slow wave while the storm raged somewhere outside in a land Hailey didn't care about at the moment.

"You thinking that you're gonna get lucky tonight, sailor?"

Hailey leaned back enough to look up into Sly's brown eyes. "Isn't that *my* line?"

Sly grinned down at her. "You weren't picking it up fast enough."

"You haven't even kissed me yet."

"Lightning," he whispered.

"What? No man has ever been this slow about kissing me before. Definitely not fast as lightning."

"Wasn't talking about that."

"What are you talking about, Surfer Boy?"

"This," and he leaned down to kiss her.

The chill of the frigid Pacific roaring outside the tavern faded away. As right as landing his helo on the pitching deck. One moment fighting the storm...

And now?

Safe on deck.

Maybe it would be her wedding next Christmas. Right here.

————

If you enjoyed this, keep reading for an excerpt from a book you're going to love.
..and a review is always welcome (it really helps)...

OFF THE LEASH

IF YOU ENJOYED THIS, YOU'LL LOVE THE
WHITE HOUSE PROTECTION FORCE
SERIES

OFF THE LEASH (EXCERPT)

WHITE HOUSE PROTECTION FORCE #1

"YOU'RE JOKING."

"Nope. That's his name. And he's yours now."

Sergeant Linda Hamlin wondered quite what it would take to wipe that smile off Lieutenant Jurgen's face. A 120mm round from an M1A1 Abrams Main Battle Tank came to mind.

The kennel master of the US Secret Service's Canine Team was clearly a misogynistic jerk from the top of his polished head to the bottoms of his equally polished boots. She wondered if the shoelaces were polished as well.

Then she looked over at the poor dog sitting hopefully on the concrete kennel floor. His stall had a dog bed three times his size and a water bowl deep enough for him to bathe in. No toys, because toys always came from the handler as a reward. He offered her a sad sigh and a liquid doggy gaze. The kennel even smelled wrong, more of sanitizer than dog. The walls seemed to echo with each bark down the long line of kennels housing the candidate hopefuls for the next addition to the Secret Service's team.

Thor—really?—was a brindle-colored mutt, part who-knew and part no-one-cared. He looked like a cross between an oversized, long-haired schnauzer and a dust mop that someone had spilled dark gray paint on. After mixing in streaks of tawny brown, they'd left one white paw just to make him all the more laughable.

And of course Lieutenant Jerk Jurgen would assign Thor to the first woman on the USSS K-9 team.

Unable to resist, she leaned over far enough to scruff the dog's ears. He was the physical opposite of the sleek and powerful Malinois MWDs—military war dogs—that she'd been handling for the 75th Rangers for the last five years. They twitched with eagerness and nerves. A good MWD was seventy pounds of pure drive—every damn second of the day. If the mild-mannered Thor weighed thirty pounds, she'd be surprised. And he looked like a little girl's best friend who should have a pink bow on his collar.

Jurgen was clearly ex-Marine and would have no respect for the Army. Of course, having been in the Army's Special Operations Forces, she knew better than to respect a Marine.

"We won't let any old swabbie bother us, will we?"

Jurgen snarled—definitely Marine Corps. Swabbie was slang for a Navy sailor and a Marine always took offense at being lumped in with them no matter how much they belonged. Of course the swabbies took offense at having the Marines lumped with *them*. Too bad there weren't any Navy around so that she could get two for the price of one. Jurgen wouldn't be her boss, so appeasing him wasn't high on her to-do list.

At least she wouldn't need any of the protective bite gear working with Thor. With his stature, he was an explosives detection dog without also being an attack one.

"Where was he trained?" She stood back up to face the beast.

"Private outfit in Montana—some place called Henderson's Ranch. Didn't make their MWD program," his scoff said exactly what he thought the likelihood of any dog outfit in Montana being worthwhile. "They wanted us to try the little runt out."

She'd never heard of a training program in Montana. MWDs all came out of Lackland Air Force Base training. The Secret Service mostly trained their own and they all came from Vohne Liche Kennels in Indiana. Unless... Special Operations Forces dogs were trained by private contractors. She'd worked beside a Delta Force dog for a single month—he'd been incredible.

"Is he trained in English or German?" Most American MWDs were trained in German so that there was no confusion in case a command word happened to be part of a spoken sentence. It also made it harder for any random person on the battlefield to shout something that would confuse the dog.

"German according to his paperwork, but he won't listen to me much in either language."

Might as well give the diminutive Thor a few basic tests. A snap of her fingers and a slap on her thigh had the dog dropping into a smart "heel" position. No need to call out *Fuss*—by my foot.

"*Pass auf!*" *Guard!* She made a pistol with her thumb and forefinger and aimed it at Jurgen as she grabbed her forearm with her other hand—the military hand sign for enemy.

The little dog snarled at Jurgen sharply enough to have him backing out of the kennel. "Goddamn it!"

"*Ruhig.*" *Quiet.* Thor maintained his fierce posture but dropped the snarl.

"*Gute Hund.*" *Good dog,* Linda countered the command.

Thor looked up at her and wagged his tail happily. She tossed him a doggie treat, which he caught midair and crunched happily.

She didn't bother looking up at Jurgen as she knelt once more to check over the little dog. His scruffy fur was so soft that it tickled. Good strength in the jaw, enough to show he'd had bite training despite his size—perfect if she ever needed to take down a three-foot-tall terrorist. Legs said he was a jumper.

"Take your time, Hamlin. I've got nothing else to do with the rest of my goddamn day except babysit you and this mutt."

"Is the course set?"

"Sure. Take him out," Jurgen's snarl sounded almost as nasty as Thor's before he stalked off.

She stood and slapped a hand on her opposite shoulder.

Thor sprang aloft as if he was attached to springs and she caught him easily. He'd cleared well over double his own height. Definitely trained...and far easier to catch than seventy pounds of hyperactive Malinois.

She plopped him back down on the ground. On lead or off? She'd give him the benefit of the doubt and try off first to see what happened.

Linda zipped up her brand-new USSS jacket against the cold and led the way out of the kennel into the hard sunlight of the January morning. Snow had brushed the higher hills around the USSS James J. Rowley Training Center—which this close to Washington, DC, wasn't saying much—but was melting quickly. Scents wouldn't carry as well on the cool air, making it more of a challenge for Thor to locate the explosives. She didn't know where they were either. The course was a test for handler as well as dog.

Jurgen would be up in the observer turret looking for any excuse to mark down his newest team. Perhaps teasing him about being just a Marine hadn't been her best tactical choice. She sighed. At least she was consistent—she'd always been good at finding ways to piss people off before she could stop herself and consider the wisdom of doing so.

This test was the culmination of a crazy three months, so she'd forgive herself this time—something she also wasn't very good at.

In October she'd been out of the Army and unsure what to do next. Tucked in the packet with her DD 214 honorable discharge form had been a flyer on career opportunities with the US Secret Service dog team: *Be all your dog can be!* No one else being released from Fort Benning that day had received any kind of a job flyer at all that she'd seen, so she kept quiet about it.

She had to pass through DC on her way back to Vermont—her parent's place. Burlington would work for, honestly, not very long at all, but she lacked anywhere else to go after a decade of service. So, she'd stopped off in DC to see what was up with that job flyer. Five interviews and three months to complete a standard six-month training course later—which was mostly a cakewalk after fighting with the US Rangers—she was on-board and this chill January day was her first chance with a dog. First chance to prove that she still had it. First chance to prove that she hadn't made a mistake in deciding that she'd seen enough bloodshed and war zones for one lifetime and leaving the Army.

The Start Here sign made it obvious where to begin, but she didn't dare hesitate to take in her surroundings past a quick glimpse. Jurgen's score would count a great deal toward where she and Thor were assigned in the future.

Mostly likely on some field prep team, clearing the way for presidential visits.

As usual, hindsight informed her that harassing the lieutenant hadn't been an optimal strategy. A hindsight that had served her equally poorly with regular Army commanders before she'd finally hooked up with the Rangers—kowtowing to officers had never been one of her strengths.

Thankfully, the Special Operations Forces hadn't given a damn about anything except performance and *that* she could always deliver, since the day she'd been named the team captain for both soccer and volleyball. She was never popular, but both teams had made all-state her last two years in school.

The canine training course at James J. Rowley was a two-acre lot. A hard-packed path of tramped-down dirt led through the brown grass. It followed a predictable pattern from the gate to a junker car, over to tool shed, then a truck, and so on into a compressed version of an intersection in a small town. Beyond it ran an urban street of gray clapboard two- and three-story buildings and an eight-story office tower, all without windows. Clearly a playground for Secret Service training teams.

Her target was the town, so she blocked the city street out of her mind. Focus on the problem: two roads, twenty storefronts, six houses, vehicles, pedestrians.

It might look normal...normalish with its missing windows and no movement. It would be anything but. Stocked with fake IEDs, a bombmaker's stash, suicide cars, weapons caches, and dozens of other traps, all waiting for her and Thor to find. He had to be sensitive to hundreds of scents and it was her job to guide him so that he didn't miss the opportunity to find and evaluate each one.

There would be easy scents, from fertilizer and diesel fuel used so destructively in the 1995 Oklahoma City bombing, to almost as obvious TNT to the very difficult to detect C-4 plastic explosive.

Mannequins on the street carried grocery bags and briefcases. Some held fresh meat, a powerful smell demanding any dog's attention, but would count as a false lead if they went for it. On the job, an explosives detection dog wasn't supposed to care about anything except explosives. Other mannequins were wrapped in suicide vests loaded with Semtex or wearing knapsacks filled with package bombs made from Russian PVV-5A.

She spotted Jurgen stepping into a glassed-in observer turret atop the corner drugstore. Someone else was already there and watching.

She looked down once more at the ridiculous little dog and could only hope for the best.

"Thor?"

He looked up at her.

She pointed to the left, away from the beaten path.

"*Such!*" Find.

Thor sniffed left, then right. Then he headed forward quickly in the direction she pointed.

———

CLIVE ANDREWS SAT IN THE SECOND-STORY WINDOW AT THE corner of Main and First, the only two streets in town. Downstairs was a drugstore all rigged to explode, except there were no triggers and there was barely enough explosive to blow up a candy box.

Not that he'd know, but that's what Lieutenant Jurgen had promised him.

It didn't really matter if it was rigged to blow for real, because when Miss Watson—never Ms. or Mrs.—asked for a "favor," you did it. At least he did. Actually, he had yet to meet anyone else who knew her. Not that he'd asked around. She wasn't the sort of person one talked about with strangers, or even close friends. He'd bet even if they did, it would be in whispers. That's just what she was like.

So he'd traveled across town from the White House and into Maryland on a cold winter's morning, barely past a sunrise that did nothing to warm the day. Now he sat in an unheated glass icebox and watched a new officer run a test course he didn't begin to understand.

Keep reading at fine retailers everywhere:
Off the Leash
...and don't forget that review. It really helps me out.

ABOUT THE AUTHOR

M.L. Buchman started the first of over 60 novels, 100 short stories, and a fast-growing pile of audiobooks while flying from South Korea to ride his bicycle across the Australian Outback. Part of a solo around the world trip that ultimately launched his writing career in: thrillers, military romantic suspense, contemporary romance, and SF/F.

Recently named in *The 20 Best Romantic Suspense Novels: Modern Masterpieces* by ALA's Booklist, they have also selected his works three times as "Top-10 Romance Novel of the Year." NPR and B&N listed other works as "Best 5 of the Year."

As a 30-year project manager with a geophysics degree who has: designed and built houses, flown and jumped out of planes, and solo-sailed a 50' ketch, he is awed by what's possible. More at: www.mlbuchman.com.

Other works by M. L. Buchman: *(* - also in audio)*

Other works by M. L. Buchman:

Contemporary Romance (cont)

Where Dreams
Where Dreams are Born
Where Dreams Reside
Where Dreams Are of Christmas
Where Dreams Unfold
Where Dreams Are Written

Science Fiction / Fantasy

Deities Anonymous
Cookbook from Hell: Reheated
Saviors 101

Single Titles
The Nara Reaction
Monk's Maze
the Me and Elsie Chronicles

Non-Fiction

Strategies for Success
Managing Your Inner Artist/Writer
*Estate Planning for Authors**
Character Voice
Narrate and Record Your Own
*Audiobook**

Short Story Series by M. L. Buchman:

Romantic Suspense

Delta Force
Delta Force

Firehawks
The Firehawks Lookouts
The Firehawks Hotshots
The Firebirds

The Night Stalkers
The Night Stalkers
The Night Stalkers 5E
The Night Stalkers CSAR
The Night Stalkers Wedding Stories

US Coast Guard
US Coast Guard

White House Protection Force
White House Protection Force

.

Contemporary Romance

Eagle Cove
Eagle Cove

Henderson's Ranch
*Henderson's Ranch**

Where Dreams
Where Dreams

Thrillers

Dead Chef
Dead Chef

Science Fiction / Fantasy

Deities Anonymous
Deities Anonymous

Other
The Future Night Stalkers
Single Titles

Printed in Great Britain
by Amazon